Praise for
EVERYONE'S GOT SOMETHING:
My First Year with Celiac Disease

"What a mitzvah! This book is such a gift to the diagnosed Celiac-ites (and eventually more to come). *Everyone's Got Something* is the perfect compilation of every topic along the first year of the gluten-free journey. PWDU should read it too! Thank you Hallie, Rayna and Lori for this fabulous book!"

—*Lisa Goldman, celiac advocate and "The Gluten Free Jewish Momma" of a college student diagnosed with celiac disease at the same age as "Lexi"*

"I like the energy that has gone into this. You guys are gonna really help people!"

—*Sheryl Harpel, mother of two teens with celiac disease and founder of Gluten Free Friends, LLC*

"WOW! This is amazing! I am so glad you wrote this! While reading it I have been alternating between smiling (in recognition of your initial spelling of "glooten") and tearing up (when Lexi's numbers go down and she jumps back on the growth curve). This is a very special book that is going to be of such help to so many people. It can definitely serve as a resource for parents as well!"

—*Dr. Michelle Daniel, psychologist who has celiac disease and is a parent to a teenager with celiac disease*

"I think this book will benefit everyone who reads it! Although I knew most of the facts, it was nice to read about someone else who went through what I went and am still going through. Lexi, the main point character, reminded me of things I experienced. For example, I also had a dream that I was eating bread the first night I was gluten free! The story is written in an easy-to-read and sometimes funny way."

—*Arielle Farber, age 12, diagnosed with celiac disease*

"Hallie and Rayna do a fantastic job transforming a daunting diagnosis into an exciting adventure. Lexi's journal is raw and real, and it gives me flashbacks to various points throughout my own celiac story. I love how Lexi puts a positive spin on her lifestyle change because it is true—everybody's got something, and we are lucky to have the only autoimmune disease whose trigger is known! I am so glad Hallie and Rayna have given the celiac community a fun, relatable story for preteens and teenagers."

—*Kelly Okun, professional golfer, diagnosed with celiac disease in 2012*

"Honest, authentic, and endlessly inspiring, *Everyone's Got Something* is an upbeat take on life with celiac—and all of the joy and beauty that can still be found despite, and because of, a life-changing diagnosis like celiac. Empowering and uplifting—and exactly what all celiac patients need to hear."

—*Jessica Press, celiac patient, mom of a celiac kid, and journalist who has written about celiac disease for Gluten-Free Living Magazine and The New York Times Education Life section*

"As someone who was diagnosed with celiac disease at age 13, I'm thrilled that these girls took on the task of writing this book at such a young age. I could only wish that I had such a book to read during my first years of being gluten free. This book is wonderfully written, incredibly relatable, and it has a little something for everyone who is on a gluten-free journey. I strongly recommend adding this book to your collection as it is truly one of a kind and a read you won't regret."

—*Taylor Miller, celiac advocate, gluten-free blogger, and co-owner of HaleLife Bakery*

EVERYONE'S GOT SOMETHING:

My First Year with Celiac Disease

WRITTEN BY:
Hallie Rose Katzman
Rayna Mae Katzman
Lori Akawie Katzman, Psy.D.

Everyone's Got Something:
My First Year with Celiac Disease

ISBN 978-1-7335992-0-7

Cover and interior design by Jera Publishing

Dedicated to
our family and
all of the "celiac-ites"
out there

Contents

FOREWORD

Hallie and Rayna Katzman, or whom I now call "the twins who will change the world," have proven over and over again that you truly can overcome any obstacle life throws at you if you have the right mindset. I feel as though I can say this with credibility because I was there from the beginning to witness firsthand what they were able to accomplish in only a few short months.

I met Hallie and Rayna while in my former role as a clinical program manager for the Kogan Celiac Center at Barnabas Health Ambulatory Care Center in Livingston, New Jersey. Their book not only describes the emotions, feelings, and thoughts someone has when they find out they have a condition that will change the way they live forever, but it also walks you through the most reliable and raw documentation of a real-life experience with celiac disease and the journey to recovery.

When I first met these two sisters, I saw myself. I too was diagnosed with celiac, and I felt many of the same emotions they did in the beginning. As I got to know them, I knew I wanted to invest in these two girls who are intelligent beyond their years and whom I could relate to. It became very evident to me after seeing them do the impossible while smiling the whole way through that they were going to use this situation for good. They did exactly that by writing this book and sharing so much of their hardship and triumph with the world.

I have seen their passion flourish even during the first year after their diagnosis. They help teach and support others, get involved with their community, raise awareness, and genuinely want to make the life of everyone with celiac disease better. By leading a food sensitivities and allergy club in their school and by being Celiac Disease Foundation Student Ambassadors, they share their knowledge and strength with their peers.

I know this is only the beginning for them, and I am certain that the "something" they were given wasn't for nothing. It is their calling, purpose, and life's work. I cannot wait to see what they will go on to accomplish, and I am honored to have a small part in their healing journey and life story.

I highly recommend this book for anyone who was recently diagnosed with celiac disease or may be struggling with the hardship that may occur because of it. We can all relate because we all have something. This book will inspire, refresh, motivate, and change you!

Nikki Yelton, RD, LDN, CNHP

Integrative & Functional Medicine Registered Dietitian Nutritionist
Celiac Disease Specialist & Former Clinical Program Manager of the
Kogan Celiac Center

INTRODUCTION

From Lori Akawie Katzman, Psy.D.

It was a Saturday afternoon in 2014 when I got the phone call from a covering physician in the pediatrician's office. That one phone call catapulted my family into a whole new way of life: learn whatever we could about celiac disease.

Our learning curve was steep and fast-paced. Our resources included our doctors, peers, and the internet, but we were also looking for an old-fashioned handheld book to read. We immediately purchased *Celiac Disease: A Hidden Epidemic*, by Dr. Peter H.R. Green and Rory Jones. Though chock-full of valuable information, it was not something my 13-year-old daughters, Rayna and Hallie, who were the ones diagnosed with the disease, would sit down to read. I came across some great illustrated picture books for younger elementary-aged kids, but only a couple of options for preteens or teens.

Much of this book was written and developed by Rayna and Hallie during that first year after they were diagnosed. While the book is fiction and told from the perspective of a character they created named Lexi, it is largely based on their firsthand and first-year experiences. In writing this book, it is our hope that newly diagnosed children and their parents will benefit from reading about the daily ups and downs of Rayna and Hallie, as told through the eyes of Lexi. It chronicles several of the "firsts" that Rayna and Hallie encountered in the doctor's office and with friends and family. The intention is that the readers feel understood, less alone, and more confident in managing this life change. Celiac disease may be part of who they are, but it does not define who they are or who they can become.

From Hallie and Rayna Katzman

Going through this journey ourselves allows us to draw from our own experiences and consider what was helpful and what was difficult and, at the end of the day, realize that it is doable! We are fully aware that each person and family will forge their own path, which may or may not resemble ours.

We know that sometimes it takes years to figure out that a loved one has celiac disease. For some people the diagnosis may be a relief; for others it can be really scary. Often people go back and forth between the two. Then there is the process of learning how to cope and live with the disease. While celiac disease may affect people differently, there's one thing that binds us all together: the only treatment is eliminating gluten. You can do this and you are not alone!

Finally, please remember that this book does not replace the medical guidance you receive from your own doctors and nutritionists. We recommend that you and your parents ask your own doctors for their medical advice about your symptoms, diagnosis, and how to take care of your health.

MY FIRST YEAR WITH CELIAC DISEASE

By Lexi

My "Well" Checkup Appointment
(Let's just say it didn't go so "well")

Dear Journal,

I'm Lexi. And you are my journal (but I think you know that already). My mom gave me this journal (you) for my 12th birthday. I didn't really see a use for you at the time, but now I think I might need you for some moral support, you know, like heart-to-hearts. I'm sitting in my bedroom while my parents are talking downstairs most likely about me and how today went. So, here's the scoop—I just turned 13. Yippee. I'm officially a teenager. Typically a cause for celebration, but today was kind of the opposite. You know the drill, with every birthday comes a visit to the doctor. Just like my first 12 years, I had my well checkup appointment with the same doctor. No shots this year—phew!—so I thought it would be easy-breezy. Oh Journal, please realize one thing: shots and I DO NOT GET ALONG. AT ALL! Yes, even bribes of everything in the

Happy Birthday to me! 13

entire world haven't worked to make this experience easier, but don't get me wrong—my mom has tried.

Anyway, this year, just like I expected, we did the regular weight and measurement routine. I grew 2 inches, gained a few pounds as usual, and blah-blah-blah. Just when I thought all was "well" and that absolutely nothing was wrong, the doctor put my measurements on my growth chart and paused. That was my first clue that all wasn't well in the Land of Lexi. On the outside I was attempting to stay calm, but on the inside there was absolute craziness.

According to the doctor, my percentiles (fancy word for percentages of people) have been getting lower and lower the past few years, starting out at the 50th to the 25th, to the 10th, to the 5th, and now I am at the 1st percentile. I am small, but pretty much I always have been, it's just how I thought I was built. I eat a lot (always have), maybe I tire a

little easier than my friends, but other than that I have been healthy (or so I think) [*insert doom music*]. My aunt always jokes to my mom that I must have a hollow leg. For the amount that I eat, she never knew where it was going [*insert more doom music*].

So based on these new, apparently "insufficient," measurements, the doctor and my mother agreed that I would get some bloodwork to make sure everything (meaning my growth) was OK.

Which brings me to sitting in my room now, writing to you. I AM NOT AT ALL HAPPY ABOUT GETTING A

BLOOD TEST! Apparently it's just a precaution, so of course I wonder WHY I really need to do this!?!?!?!? Did I mention that I DO NOT LIKE BLOOD TESTS (ok, I never really had one, but if it's anything like getting a shot, I. AM. NOT. A. FAN.)

Thanks for listening—I may be onto something with this journal-writing thing,

Lexi

The Blood Test

Dear Journal,

Well, we went ahead with the bloodwork. Even with the lidocaine—the cream my mom got me to numb a spot on my arm—I was still terrified of the needle. A few years ago, my mom read about athletes using lidocaine to numb their skin. (Just so you know, my mom reads A LOT, and whatever she can pass onto me, she does. She sends me texts and emails with links to articles, and sometimes she even prints them out for me. It can be annoying sometimes—ok, a lot of the time—but other times I feel lucky that she cares. That's just some side info for you, Journal.)

Anyway, Mom asked my doctor to prescribe the lidocaine. In my head I know the needle doesn't really hurt, but I just get SOOOOO nervous about it. I mean does anyone really like getting shots or bloodwork!? No one I know.

LIDOCAINE

For your information, my throat has finally healed from the screaming. As I said, I'm really not one for shots or anyone poking me, but I'm over it. I can't say as much for the phlebotomist (the guy who took my blood). I may have caused him temporary hearing loss. I'm serious. Completely serious. My mom said I won't always want or feel like I need the lidocaine … She's just "indulging" me to get me over this hump.

To be continued (without a numb spot on my arm),

Lexi

MAY 1

The Blood Results

Dear Journal,

It's Thursday, and I was just eating a bowl of pretzels, my normal after-school snack. I mean, doesn't everyone have this one snack that they're just completely obsessed with?! Yeah, so mine is pretzels... Anyway, Mom starts watching me eating my pretzels with this serious look on her face. She starts with "Lexi... Honey...," and I'm already feeling my stomach churn because when a parent uses two names they're usually trying to sugarcoat something. And I hate sugarcoating stuff!!!!!! (unless they're pretzels dipped in chocolate—now that's something to sugarcoat).

Okay, back on track. So, my mom continued by saying something about high numbers on my blood test, squished intestines, something called glootin in the food I was eating, changing some of the food I was eating, not growing, and Sillyack Disease. I was just sitting there like WHAT?! I

8

had already forgotten about the blood test, let alone the fact that we were waiting for results! Isn't the phrase "No news is good news"? I just didn't realize that my mom had already gotten the news.

My mom came over, hugged me, and told me that everything would be okay. I believed her (you haven't met my mom, but she is basically right about EVERYTHING, and even when she isn't right, she points out that "no one is perfect" to make sure I don't feel bad when I do mess up and all of that wonderful positive stuff). But, I have to tell you, Journal, on the inside, I was ALL OVER THE PLACE AND FREAKING OUT. I still am! Seriously, I'm a little confused about this new information, a little excited (about eating new food), more than a little nervous (about eating new food), and at the same time very much freaking out (about eating new food)!

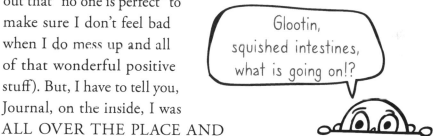

Glootin, squished intestines, what is going on!?

I tried to keep my cool (which is kind of difficult) and take it all in. Then, my mom's eyes went down to the bowl of pretzels, and I could tell just from that look that I would have to find a new after-school snack. It was in that moment that my once-loved pretzels no longer had their appeal anymore, especially if they were causing me to have squished intestines and not grow as well as I could. I used my pinky finger to shove the bowl away, and I came up here to spill my guts to you. (No pun intended.) Guts, a.k.a. my intestines—thanks 5th-grade science class.

To be continued ... Gotta go have a "Family Discussion" about this Sillyack Disease.

WTYL (Write To You Later). Wish me luck!
Lexi

MAY 2

The Pediatric Gastroenterologist, a.k.a. the G.I. Guy

Dear Journal,

My mom acted quickly. Even before she told me about the blood results, she had already scheduled an appointment with a new doctor. That's where I am now. In the waiting room of this new doctor, called a gastroenterologist (I copied that from the fancy name plate on his door), which is a little intimidating and scary. According to my mom, the gastroenterologist (let's call him the G.I. Guy) is a doctor who helps people with their digestion issues—their stomach and intestines. Just another word to add to my colossal (another big word) vocabulary. I already met him, but once he and my parents started talking about an endoscopy (another big word), it seemed to be a good idea for me to get a little air. So I came out into the waiting room while the G.I. Guy and my parents had their own heart-to-heart.

When I first met the G.I. Guy he was fine and all (no shots, just measurements—everyone is oddly interested in my height and weight). He was super professional, but things went a little

Dr. G.I. Guy
GASTROENTEROLOGIST

south for me when he kept calling something "ABNORMAL." I couldn't tell if he was referring to me, or to my intestines, or to my bloodwork. He was like, "This is very abnormal. You see, we must fix this very abnormal problem as soon as possible. Very abnormal..." Seriously, that's what he said. I don't think I will ever forget those sentences.

And then he and my parents talked FOREVER about my "abnormal" guts as I sat there listening. They kept talking about this Sillyack Disease, that glootin stuff my mom was telling me about, and whether or not I was getting an endoscopy. I had NO idea what that was, but I had a feeling it was not going to be on my top 10 list of most fun things to do this summer. I'm pretty sure that my mom saw the panic on my face because she put down her own notepad and pen and suggested I go wait outside a few minutes, which brings me to writing in you.

I came into this office an innocent girl, and I seem to be leaving it an "abnormal" girl with Sillyack Disease. Thanks for the new label, G.I. Guy. Apparently, the bloodwork revealed numbers that we were not only "abnormal," but, in fact, "<u>very</u> abnormal." I don't know about you, but I am 13 years old, in 7th grade, smack in the middle of middle school, going to 2 Bat and Bar Mitzvahs a weekend. Don't you think the doctor could have come up with another way to say that my test results were totally high and out of whack? Because, really, what's "normal" for a brand-new teenager?! What's normal for a 13-year-old? Or should I say, what's NOT abnormal for a 13-year-old? We are like in that in-between stage of growing up. One day we want to curl up next to our parents and read a book, and the next day we are slamming our bedroom door if we think someone looks at us funny. So while "abnormal" may not have been the best word for the doctor to choose, it certainly seems to be sending my parents into some serious A-C-T-I-O-N.

I guess I will be taking action too, but while they are still sitting in the office with the G.I. Guy I am left here thinking about how life can really change itself in a matter of seconds, Journal. Like I could start writing in another pen and your pages would be changed forever. **Hi, Journal. How do you like this??? Huh? NOBODY LIKES CHANGE, but sometimes you have to deal with it. That's exactly what I'm going to do with Sillyack. Turn it around and make it good!! First step is finding out more about it and what in the world glootin is. I'm going to attempt to ignore the endoscopy thing for now, but** first things first, I am going to stop writing in that Sharpie and return it to the reception desk because it certainly left its mark and went through a bunch of my pages! UGH!

Thanks for letting me vent!

Lexi
♡

So What Is Gluten?
(With a Little Help from
Jimmy Kimmel)

Dear Journal,

Here's another vocabulary word to add to your ever-growing list:

GLUTEN, not glootin

Whoops! My dad looked it up on the computer and saw that Jimmy Kimmel—yes, the late-night talk show host—did a funny video on his show about gluten. He interviewed all of these fit, healthy-looking people outside their gym and asked them, "What is gluten?" No one he interviewed knew what it really was, but EVERYONE was claiming NOT to eat it. It would have been really funny if it wasn't so important to me to figure out what it is!! Ok, it was still funny—it's Jimmy Kimmel! But here is an FYI:

having Sillyack means
I NEED to go gluten free!

It's not to stay fit like these Jimmy Kimmel interviewees think they are doing. No gluten anytime, anywhere, ever... Talk about hard!

Let me take the mystery out of the "What is gluten?" question. DUN-DUN-DUN!!! It's a protein that sort of acts like glue and helps food hold its shape and stay together. It is found mostly in 3 grains—wheat, barley, and rye—but wait, it also comes disguised in other ingredients [*insert doom music*]. Apparently it's like a chameleon and sneaks into a lot of foods that you wouldn't expect. For example, Twizzlers and KitKats are a no-go, but regular Hershey Kisses, Tootsie Rolls, and Jelly Belly jelly beans are safe to eat. Phew! LOVE, LOVE, LOVE jelly beans!

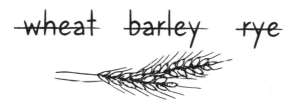

So foods with gluten in them cause problems for people with Sillyack Disease. The gluten attacks these things called villi, which are on our small intestine. They help a person absorb the food they are eating, but when they are attacked by the gluten, they don't work as well—cue in the squished intestines issue and not getting the nutrition from the food you thought you were. True story.

At the end of you, Journal, I am going to start making a list of safe foods that I can eat. I will include certain things to watch out for too if I forget, but focus more on what I CAN have—better to see the glass half full than half empty.

FUN FACT: I just learned in science class that the glass is really always full because there is air in it, too!

Going down to the kitchen to get some gluten-less food,
Lexi

MAY II

What I've Learned So Far

Dear Journal,

It's only been a few days since my appointment with the G.I. Guy, and here's what I've learned so far:

1) Oops! It's not spelled SILLYACK—it is CELIAC. My bad, I was just writing it like I heard it, hahaha. Mom gave me an article—got it!

2) I can eat everything that does NOT have gluten in it (or wheat, rye, or barley—oats, by the way are not recommended for the first year, so I'm staying clear of them for now).

3) I can eat everything that has NOT TOUCHED gluten (or wheat, rye, barley, or oats). If it touches, that is an issue!!

4) Once I start eating only foods without gluten, my small intestine will heal and the little villi will start to work again for me, so I will get nourishment from the food I am eating, AND I SHOULD GROW(!!!!). See, my celiac symptom was "short stature." Some people get really,

really, really bad stomach pains or get foggy and can't think straight. My mom showed me this article (remember I told you she reads a lot) that said there are around 200–300 DIFFERENT SYMPTOMS that are linked with celiac disease—that is A LOT of possible symptoms.

200 to 300 Different Symptoms!!!

5) It's also the most undiagnosed genetic disease there is, which means A LOT of people have it and don't realize they have it. My mom said that will be changing because the doctors are testing for it more now, and a lot more people will be finding out they have it, like me. (Oh joy, join the club!!)

Lexi

18

MAY 13

Telling My Friends

Dear Journal,

Today I told my friends at school. It was like a great reveal of this big secret I had inside of me (literally). I couldn't wait to tell them. I started with the scary:

"I-have-an-announcement-so-you-better-stop-talking"

speech. My friends started screaming out things at me like "I'll be your bridesmaid!" or "No don't move, you can live with me!" or the standard "I'll be there for you!" even before they knew what I was talking about. That's my friends—they are good friends and generally caring people. It took me all of 2 seconds to regain their attention. I was all like "I (dramatic pause) have celiac!"

Ok, the dramatic pause part was just in my head—it didn't really happen like that. Instead, I acted semi-calm and just announced it. Their reactions were calm, and they were all quiet for a few seconds, which felt like a few minutes, but I could see they were taking in the information. Not much can quiet up a group of 13-year-old girls at lunch time, but this did for a moment. Inside I was like, "YESSSSSS THEY UNDERSTAND ME," and I am so happy to get this off my chest! On the outside I'm in answering-questions-with-a-serious-face mode. I was overwhelmed.

FRIEND: "So you can't have bread?"

ME: "That and wheat, rye, and barley."

FRIEND: "Oh, well that stinks."

ME: "Actually it's good that they found it now rather than later. I sort of haven't been growing as well as I should have been. I'm lucky to know now."

FRIEND: "I know someone else who has it. She's doing ok. Let me know if you want to talk."

This one was followed by a hug—that was the best one. Then it was over. Pretty quickly everyone was back to the normal talking about too much homework, the big science test we have coming up, and loving ga-ga in gym. Ga-ga is awesome and I can play it with or without celiac. Unfortunately I can do my homework, too. Celiac changes some things, but not everything.

Now I have to do my gluten-free homework! Kidding, that's naturally gluten free!

Lexi

MAY 17

An En-What?

Dear Journal,

So, apparently there is this thing that I may or may not need called an ENDOSCOPY. AAAAHHHH!!! Remember when I first met the G.I. Guy, and he was talking about it with my parents? I guess I purposefully erased it from my brain. Not hard to do—I had lots of other new information to fill it up with. So yesterday, my parents explained what it is, and I AM SCARED. I asked my friends what they think of this non-sense—only one of them has actually had one. She said she felt the same way as me and that it was kind of scary to think about, but she didn't remember it being too much of a big deal. She said the doctors put you to sleep while they do the procedure. The endoscopy is actually done so the doctor can take a biopsy (or a sample) of your intestines. All in all, she explained it to be an OK experience, which is good information to have, very good information. My mom said it is the "GOLD" standard of diagnosing celiac (there goes her reading again—sometimes I like what she reads and sometimes I don't).

Endoscopy = the "GOLD" standard to diagnose

As you know, I HATE people poking me, so I REALLY don't want an endoscopy. Oh well, my parents are crystal clear on my likes and dislikes, so maybe that'll affect their decision ... They are talking about it right now as I write to you. AAAAH!!!!!!! I was just called down for a family discussion!!!!!! Be right back ...

 TEN MINUTES LATER ...

DRUM ROLL PLEASE!!!! I am not having an endoscopy! This time my abnormally high numbers came through for me in a backwards sort of way.

Although an endoscopy is HIGHLY, HIGHLY, HIGHLY recommended, my parents and the G.I. Guy decided at that appointment when I left the room that if my parents are tested for celiac and one of them shows up with something then it will "further support my ABNORMALLY high numbers." DRUMROLL PLEASE AGAIN ... It turns out that while I was at school my parents got tested. My dad has the DQ8 gene, and my mom has the DQ2 gene and one of her blood levels was slightly elevated. BA-BAM! NO endoscopy for me! Well, it is a genetic disease, which means if one of my parents had one of the genes, then I could too. Apparently, my parents are so efficient: they each had one of the genes and here you go—a daughter with celiac was born.

It's really NOT as simple or straightforward as that because apparently you can have the gene and not have celiac, but all things were pointing in the direction for me that yes indeed I HAVE CELIAC DISEASE. Remember my numbers were ABNORMALLY HIGH. So here's the thing: the ABNORMALLY HIGH numbers indicate that my body is viewing gluten as a threat. It's like the gluten, which is typically an acceptable thing for people to eat, is an unwanted alien in my body, and in my case the ABNORMALLY HIGH NUMBERS show that there is an injury to my small intestine.

With that said, we are going full steam ahead—<u>without the gluten</u>.

I am really happy I don't have to have the endoscopy, but based on what my friend explained to me, it doesn't seem that bad to have it anymore (but let's keep that a secret between you and me). In all seriousness, I've had a full plate lately. I was bat mitzvahed 4 weeks ago, had the school nurse think I had scoliosis 3 weeks ago (followed by a visit to the doctor and an x-ray to rule it out), had 6 teeth pulled out 2 weeks ago by the oral surgeon (that was U.G.L.Y. for me, my mom, the oral surgeon and his assistant, and anyone else in the office at the time), and got braces last week! I'm trying to handle all of these events with a smile, but it hurts to smile (thanks, braces). Seriously though, enough is enough for now. Thanks, Mom and Dad, for taking this one off my plate, especially for taking the gluten off my plate!

WTYL,

Lexi

MAY 18

Going Gluten Free

Dear Journal,

I like pancakes. I wish I could end my sentence there, but there is actually more to this journal entry ... HAHA. Back to pancakes. Based on what my parents and doctors say, my small intestine is not supposed to look like one. After we saw the Jimmy Kimmel video, they pulled up a picture on the internet of what they were guessing my small intestine looked like. They said a pancake. I thought to myself it looked more like a kugel (a flat noodle dish we eat on the holidays).

Anyway, if I follow the prescription from the G.I. Guy—eat gluten free so the little villi grow back and my small intestine returns to looking more like a sponge with coral growing on it and can catch the nutrients from food and absorb them into my body—I should grow and feel better. So basically I don't want pancakes (or kugel) growing in me, but I do want a sponge-like coral organ growing in my body. Depending on the amount of damage that has been done, it will take time to heal, maybe 6 months to a year or even 2. Well, fortunately I'm only 13, so I have time . . .

Mine

flat villi

What it should be

healthy villi

So, the Land of Lexi has met Celiac World, the land of gluten-free food! It shouldn't be THAT bad. There are <u>tons</u> of replacements for food, and some of my favorite foods (apples, corn, rice, and fruit smoothies) were even gluten free before (we just didn't even realize it because I guess we didn't have to)!

OK Journal, you are going to be my honorary "celiac-ite" on this journey! Be honored. Be very honored. This is gonna be a fun one.

Lexi (Supreme Ruler of the Celiac-ites)

Nicole the Nutritionist—
She ROCKS!

Dear Journal,

2 hours! Yes, 2 hours—that's how much time we just spent with a nutritionist. It was totally worth it, she was AH-MAY-ZINGGGG!!!!!!!! I didn't know what to expect. I've never been to an expert to talk about food before this crazy experience, but it felt like going to a doctor (except she wasn't a doctor) that didn't poke, prod, or demand that you get a shot. Instead she talked, asked questions, really listened to my answers, and let us ask questions, and oh boy, did my mom have questions... She even schlepped 2 bags of food from our house to go over the ingredients with Nicole to see what was okay and what was not. Nicole was SOOOOO patient and she just listened, which we really needed, and she gave us a huge basket of GF treats to take home to sample. (GF is gluten free, but I probably didn't have to tell you that.)

GF = gluten free

I feel pretty inspired and armed with information. My mind is in overload mode with celiac info. I just want to read 1 million food labels!! Yes, it is completely clear to me that I can't eat my beloved whole wheat crackers anymore that I literally have every morning for breakfast, but I'll find something else.

Nicole herself was diagnosed with celiac when she was in college. She was sick for many years, and no one knew what was going on. Her life changed for the better when she went gluten free. Change is scary (as you know from the scarring Sharpie experience, Journal—sorry about that . . .), but she didn't get sick anymore, and she had more energy—those seem like pretty inviting changes.

Well, it's not entirely true that she never got sick again. She did tell us about a time that she got "glutened," which means without realizing it she ate something that had gluten in it while at a friend's house. She said some people "feel" the gluten right away, but she said it hit her about an hour and a half later, and when it did, she felt terrible, just awful.

◎ TIPS WHEN "GLUTENED":

- Talk to your doctor or nutritionist about options so you are ready if or when it happens
- Drink lots of water
- Find out about nausea medication
- Get rest and sleep
- Give yourself some love and accept care from others
- Don't blame yourself, accidents happen
- Try to remember you will eventually feel better

She told us about nausea medication that some doctors prescribe for people when they are "glutened." She said staying hydrated and taking the medicine can help avoid the full impact that the gluten has, but since symptoms are so different from person to person, she really recommends following up with a doctor. But, I'll tell you, getting "glutened" doesn't sound fun. NOT. AT. ALL. Unfortunately, it seems like it can happen even when you are trying to be super careful, but hopefully it doesn't happen a lot.

I'm not sure if I'll feel getting "glutened"—some people say that once the gluten is cleared from my body, I may feel it and that's scary to me. I'm not looking forward to it, but I'm really grateful I met Nicole. I can tell she's going to be an important person to help me learn how to live with this disease and make healthy decisions for myself. I'm kind of excited, kind of nervous, too, but I'm ready. I can't wait to go food shopping and check out some labels. I'm sort of nervous. Did I mention I'm excited?!

Converting the Kitchen

Dear Journal,

I didn't really have a hand in the kitchen conversion. I was more of an innocent bystander watching my mom do a complete overhaul. EVERYTHING AND I MEAN EVERYTHING was washed in the dishwasher, and the drawers and cabinets were cleaned so no crumbs were left in sight or out of sight for that matter.

NOT SO FUN FACT: One crumb of bread contains about 24 to 30 mg of gluten. For some people that can cause symptoms and intestinal damage (remember my mom reads A LOT)!

At the suggestion of our fabulous nutritionist we got a new toaster, cutting board, colander, wooden spoons, and even new pots and pans. My mom did a complete kitchen utensil makeover, and she washed everything that we kept in the dishwasher 2 times.

> BIG DISCLAIMER: Most families don't go as overboard as my mom, but the whole CROSS-CONTAMINATION thing was freaking her out a bit, so let's just say the gluten in my house is history, as in see ya later, adios non mi amigo gluten.

Nicole said some celiac families have people in their house who can eat gluten, so they have separate toasters, labeled containers, and certain foods that are just for the person with celiac to eat. It's a family decision—you either keep it all gluten free even for the people that can have gluten, which can upset the gluten eaters, or you keep gluten and gluten-free food in the house, which will require some good organization, like separate drawers and top shelves for the gluten-free foods and items. It is doable. Everybody's got to live and figure out how to make it work for their family—the brothers, sisters, and adults. My family is making it easy for me by making it a completely gluten-free household, but I have to imagine that this isn't always the case.

Mom also explained to me that people respond to having this disease differently, sort of like religion. The beauty of religion is that you figure out what you believe in and what makes sense to you. The same for celiac—there are clear guidelines and no-no's, but there are also different levels of observances. Mom says we are "conservative celiacs." I get it, we are strict. But … there are positives to that, like my intestines absorbing nutrients and me growing.

Writing to you from my super-clean, gluten-less kitchen,
Lexi

Finding Replacement Foods for Favorite Foods—
BREAD IS NOT DEAD

Dear Journal,

OMG OMG OMG OMG OMG!!! ~~Food shopping~~ Eating new foods is officially my favorite activity. I mean who would not like sampling the best GF foods on the face of the planet?? Ok, Journal, you might be wondering, "Where did Lexi get all of this food excitement from?" A lot of reality cooking shows and the real answer: AMAZING GF FOOD REPLACEMENTS!!!! So remember how I was obsessed with pretzels? Well, have no fear, Glutino is here!! They make the best GF pretzels ever! Also pizza? Forget about it. Udis has it 10000000% covered.

Then there's bread. Well I thought that would be the hardest, but I have a friend whose mom knows A LOT about celiac, and BREAD IS NOT DEAD everyone, let me tell you! She

started this gluten-free Google group and is a big advocate for homemade bread. In minutes, she taught my mom how to use this miracle-working bread maker. It literally kneads, mixes, and bakes the bread for you. So of course we got it for Mom for Mother's Day. And it makes the yummiest bread that doesn't even taste like bread. It's like cake!! Seriously, it's that good. When my friends are over I'm lucky if I get a slice for myself. I can't thank this woman enough—THANKS FOR HELPING MY MOM HELP ME!

And for desserts, look for GF places near you! I was able to find two, one a grain-free bakery and the other a dedicated GF bakery. Both are AMAZINGLY AWESOME!!! So if someone asks me, "Can you have (fill in any type of food)?" I just say, "Yeah, gluten-free style!" Which is a totally awesome thing to be able to say. I've replaced my morning crackers with a GF cereal as I haven't found a cracker that really makes me happy, but I'll keep looking. I won't lie to you, finding substitutes for the pretzels, chips, and brownies that we love took a bit of trial and error, but believe it or not the pasta, pizza, and bagels we eat now I like better than B.C. (Before Celiac). So … THANK YOU TO ALL OF THE COMPANIES THAT MAKE GLUTEN-FREE FOOD BECAUSE YOU MAKE PEOPLE'S LIVES SOOOOO MUCH EASIER!!!!!!! Ok, I think you get how much I love GF food.

WTYL,
Lexi

Celiac Support Group

Dear Journal,

I went to my first celiac support group. It was headed by my rock-star nutritionist, Nicole. There weren't a lot of kids, but I hit if off right away with another girl my age. It turns out she had a similar story to mine—no tummy symptoms, just small for her age and really, really, really high numbers on her bloodwork. The crazy thing she told me was that after her endoscopy in the hospital, they offered her a piece of pound cake to eat. Can you believe it—pound cake! And not the gluten-free kind. She happily had it, and I'm pretty sure that was her last bit of gluten-filled food because her small intestine was of the gluten-filled pancake variety—flat.

Back to the meeting. The room was full of people who had celiac—they were mostly adults and were generally diagnosed later in life. They had other health issues like anemia and osteoporosis from not being diagnosed for so many years. My mom said we were lucky that we found out about the celiac disease now or else it could have led to other issues down the road. It's really hard to think about things down the road. I mean I'm only 13, but I'll take my mom's word for it.

In any case, it was really nice to be with a room full of people who all have celiac—everyone was friendly and wanted to know my name, and they all looked happy to be together. I initially felt pretty nervous, but I wound up feeling more glad than nervous when I was there. That was pretty cool. I'll definitely go to another meeting.

Lexi

Yes, There Is a Gluten-Free Expo

Dear Journal,

I went to a gluten-free expo! Yes, you read that right. Most people have heard of car expos or flower expos, but what do you know?! There is a gluten-free expo, and I was surrounded by gluten-free goodness everywhere. Actually, it's called the Gluten Free and Allergy Friendly Expo—GFAF, for short. There were tables and tables and tables of people promoting their gluten-free products—food, makeup, lotions, seasonings, magazines, and more. I sort of felt like a kid in a candy store, but my mom was still super cautious about me trying things. There were hands everywhere, and she was anxious about the cross-contamination thing.

It was still awesome to be there with so many people who believed in their products and supported being gluten free. I left with 2 bags full of new foods to try and a lip gloss. Good idea whoever made the lip gloss—I didn't think that would

36

be an important to thing to have to avoid getting "glutened," but it really is. On our way out my dad entered us into a raffle to go to a gluten-free family camp for a weekend. Cross your fingers and your toes—that could be fun!

Lexi

My First Gluten-Free Baking Experience Was Just About As Flat As My Small Intestine

Dear Journal,

So we had this assignment for my LAR class (that's short for Language Arts and Reading). We got to bake and had to label our food with alliteration. Yes, I am in 7th grade, yes I go to a regular public school, and yes this was an unusual assignment, but anyway I was all set to make "Blissful Blueberry Muffin Bites." I was pretty excited, as it turns out my teacher has celiac disease, too, so I thought it would be great to bring in something she could eat.

Well, can you say EPIC FAIL!? I'm guessing that my nerves got the best of me. Round 1 of baking turned out to be a complete disaster. I was nervous—it was my first time baking gluten free. My proportions and measurements must have been totally off, but my mom kept her act together. We stood in the kitchen looking over a bowl of gritty, dry batter that turned into gritty, dry, flat muffins. She tried one and said, "Maybe this is what gluten-free muffins look like. I would eat these." Thanks for the positivity, Mom, but seriously, EW!!!

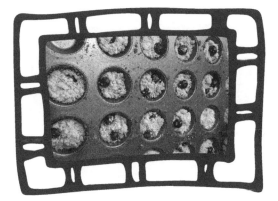

Then she suggested we give it a second try. After a deep breath and being a bit more careful with the measuring cup, voila! I made some moist, fluffy muffins that rivaled any "regular" muffins out there! EPIC FAILS OFTEN LEAD TO EPIC WINS. But seriously, it was pretty funny and will make for a good story down the road, but lesson learned—pay attention to the measurements when baking. Whew! I'm happy that I don't have to eat the first ones.

Round 1 < Round 2!

Never give up,

JUNE 19

It's a Pool Party

Dearest Journal,

Today, I'm in a good mood!!! I'm going to my friend's end-of-the-year pool party, and I'm SOOOO excited! When I got the invite I was like YESSS, and as I read, toward the bottom it said, "Snacks will be served." I was then thinking "NOOO!" I mean, it's my first big outing involving food pretty much since the whole celiac diagnosis happened. I did have a few bar and bat mitzvahs, but the parties were so late at night; I always ate something even before I went GF. But now, this pool party is here, and there is a definite in-my-face food issue. I still wish I could snack like the rest of my friends. I know I'm going to feel left out a little bit, but I also know I can't eat what will be served. Instead I'm going to focus on what I CAN have and what I CAN do. Remember, it's a pool party—I can swim regardless of the food situation!

Anyway, my mom is packing me a small bag with some delicious GF pretzels (MUCH better than non-GF pretzels), some sliced cucumbers, and a brownie. It might feel a little weird to bring my own food, but I'm deciding that it's just one of those things, and it's as weird as you make it. I'll bring a little extra in case someone wants a taste. Okay, not the cucumbers, but the pretzels and brownies are really good!

TIP: Call before you go!

My mom called the host to find out what was being served so she can send me with similar food, just the GF version. That way I sort of blend in and I know what yummy stuff to bring! And, just to make sure things go as smoothly as possible, my mom and I reviewed "being a good guest." If they (the hosts) bought me some GF food, but put it in a cross-contaminated bowl or if a lot of other hands were dipping into the bowl after eating gluten-filled food, then I'll be very thank you-ey and appreciative and then eventually eat my own stuff (not theirs, even though it would be VERY, VERY, VERY nice of them to buy special food for me!).

I gotta go pack my bag! It's sort of like having a safe picnic!

WTYL,
Lexi

P.S. I'm back home, and overall, the pool party was a SUCCESS!

Swimming ✓
Laughing ✓
Eating ✓

No, it wasn't fun not being able to eat what everyone else had, but I made do with what I brought. Nobody looked at me funny or made any comments about me bringing myself something to eat. And yes, I was right about the pretzels—it was a good thing I had enough for myself and to pass some around to my friends. They LOVE the crunch!

Being Kosher Helps

Dear Journal,

I live in a traditional kosher-style household. We have 2 sets of dishes and silverware, we don't mix meat and dairy, and don't eat any types of shellfish—the basics. There are rules and I follow them. It's just the way it is and always has been for me.

I know not everyone is Jewish and I know that not all Jewish people are kosher and I know that many other people are much more kosher than me, but this is how my family does it. Being kosher was new for my dad when he got married to my mom, and she had to sell him on it. She did—he may not like it all of the time, but he does it. But for me I think being kosher not only reminds me about being Jewish every day, but it has taught me to think about what I'm eating and when I'm eating and to be careful. My mom thinks this has helped me transition a little more easily to the gluten-free world. I've always paid some attention to what I'm eating, and obviously there have been some restrictions, like no bacon or cheeseburgers. Yes, Journal you can pick up your jaw—I know some of my friends can't believe it either, but that's just not what we do.

True, there are a lot more rules now, but I guess thinking before I eat is not all brand-new to me. I suppose someone who is a vegetarian or a pescatarian or has a food allergy might get what I'm talking about.

The most important thing is not to cheat. It may be hard, but being gluten free will help me now and in the long run.

Got to think before you eat,
Lexi

Eating Out with My
SEVERE ALLERGY DINING CARD

Dear Journal,

The trickiest thing so far has been going out to eat. IT'S SO
ANNOYING! If I were to live the rest of my life in my mom's
kitchen, life would be easy-breezy, but like my mom said, that
is not living in the "real world." We haven't been too adven-
turous so far as we are working hard for my small intestine to
heal and my bloodwork numbers to get to a "normal" level.
Even so, we have found a couple of local restaurants that can
serve me gluten-free food prepared safely. The thing is eating
GF is pretty popular now, and A LOT of people are choosing
to eat GF because they have a sensitivity to gluten or they
think it's healthier, but that is not the case for people with
celiac disease—we HAVE to eat that way, and there is a whole
cross-contamination issue. So if a restaurant offers GF pasta,
but cooks it in the pot they just made regular pasta in, then
that is a MAJOR NO-NO and can be bad for us celiac-ites.

TIP:
Dining cards can be found on the internet in so many languages. Great for traveling!

So I need to find restaurants that take the cross-contamination issue seriously and that GET IT … This is where the SEVERE ALLERGY DINING CARD I got from Nicole and ASKING QUESTIONS come into play. My mom made a gazillion copies of the card to give to the waiter or manager at whatever restaurant we go to. That person (hopefully) will pass it on to the chef. It basically says in big bold letters that I have a severe food allergy and celiac disease and lists the ingredients I cannot eat, what I can eat, and where hidden sources of gluten may be found. This has been the most successful way for us to feel comfortable eating out and is a good opening for us to ask the questions we have. My mom found similar cards on the internet that can be printed out, too!

The part that I'm trying to wrap my head around is that I am not actually ALLERGIC to gluten, but the "regular" person gets what an ALLERGY is much more easily than what celiac disease is, and if that is what gets their attention and makes it possible for me to eat out safely, then that is what I will do.

Some people are allergic to wheat and they react physically, but people with celiac have what my mom told me is an "autoimmune condition"—the gluten basically attacks the small intestine. It's SO RUDE of the gluten, but that's what it does. Eating the gluten can cause some symptoms in people right away or after a few minutes or a few hours, OR you can feel nothing at all, but it causes lots of damage on your insides over time.

It reminds me of that picture of the flat intestine my parents showed me ... I want the coral-like sponge version (insert smiley face), so if I have to use an allergy card to get there, I will.

Handing the waiter an allergy card is a good way to begin a conversation about the menu. You have to ask questions, and they can vary depending on where you are eating and what you want to eat ... FYI, we tried a Korean restaurant, and we were able to print out an allergy/celiac disease dining card in Korean from the internet!!! That was super helpful.

So the questions ... There's a list of restaurant questions that I started putting together at the end of you, Journal. It takes time to ask them. It definitely feels a little embarrassing, but it's a necessity. I know the more I do it, the more confident I'll become. And oh, that's the silver lining—I'm learning to speak up for myself. Truthfully, it doesn't always work out—over the phone, one restaurant manager basically told my dad that we shouldn't come if we were concerned about celiac disease. Even though they had a gluten-free menu, the manager admitted their kitchen was not equipped to handle cross-contamination issues. We went somewhere else.

Lexi

AUGUST 27

Dreams

Dear Journal,

The weirdest thing in the world just happened to me. I just woke up from a very, very off-putting dream, and I'm still a little out of it. I was eating a SANDWICH. I don't remember what kind of sandwich, but it was on WHOLE WHEAT BREAD!!!!! And I couldn't stop eating it. I knew I wasn't supposed to eat it, but for some unknown reason I kept eating it anyway!!! I'm still grossed out. It was just one of those dreams that felt so real ... which has given me the official creeps. Ok, well I know it's not true now so I am taking a major deep breath. Thanks for listening ... Now I sound like a radio announcer.

TOP STORY

Girl has dream of eating gluten and freaks out.

That's a top story for sure.

Gotta go contact the local news,
Lexi

49

Supermarkets

(You name it, my parents have been there)

Dear Journal,

You know the stereotype: teenage girls are supposed to love malls, parties, and salons. Well, I know some who do and others who like to be on the baseball field or tennis court, drawing, or in the debate club, but let me tell you about this teenage girl's new favorite—SUPERMARKETS!!! Literally every market in the 30-mile radius around my house my parents have visited. At first I didn't want to go, fearing I would be tempted by all the foods I couldn't eat, but it's actually like a scavenger hunt. You get to explore all the shelves on a quest for that beloved certified GF sign. And oh my gosh I'll tell you I LOVE LOVE LOVE that symbol. My mom's eyes light up when she sees it, it's like Christmas for her, and she doesn't even celebrate Christmas!

Some markets have aisles marked gluten free, but we decided not to be limited by that—there are GF options throughout the stores, and then again there are unprocessed, naturally GF foods in ALL stores, which Nicole has often pointed out are healthier for me. No matter what, there is a lot of GF goodness to be found! It's a win-win situation! My small intestine wins and so does my stomach! The only thing that loses is my parents' credit card as processed packaged items tend to be pricey. We are experimenting and I'm not afraid to try new foods. Even without wheat, rye, and barley, food can be awesome! Side note: It's even better when my dad goes to the market without my mom. You can almost guarantee that he will find a new food—he's like a GF dessert magnet!

Lexi

OCTOBER 14

Follow-Up Blood Tests

Dear Journal,

I HATE THEM. Always HAVE, PROBABLY ALWAYS WILL even though my grandpa who is a doctor told me my "right antecubital space is beautiful." There's a big word for you—antecubital space. Yup, that's the spot in front of the elbow where they stick the needle in.

On the plus side, I cry a little less each time, but it is what it is. I am not a fan of needles or blood tests even with the lidocaine. I just hate them. Maybe one day it will be better for me. It is good to have hope. The silver lining is that my "abnormal" numbers went down a little bit. Moving in the right direction—phew—but I still hate them. Just being completely honest. I truly hate them, but I know I have to do them.

Lexi

The Good Moments
(Thoughtful family and friends, finding yummy gf food)

Dear Journal,

MY EXTENDED FAMILY HAS BEEN AH-MAY-ZING! They totally get it. From getting new cutting boards, colanders, and sponges, to even buying a separate pot to cook in, I really, really, really appreciate them making me feel comfortable and having food for me that's safe to eat. I have the best family ever! From the cookbook that my aunt sent me, to the magazine and book my other aunt sent me, to my younger cousin literally asking if everything SHE was eating was GF because she wanted to support me and understand what was going on: I AM LUCKY!

MY FRIENDS HAVE BEEN A.W.E.S.O.M.E. They compliment my GF food A LOT! There's something about my pretzels everybody loves, and when I go to my friends' houses, on more than one occasion their moms have made sure I have something safe to eat. A friend even ordered a meal for me from a "safe" restaurant, and another friend chose to have her birthday dinner at a restaurant she knew I could easily eat at. That was over-the-top nice of her! Other friends have a spot in their kitchen just for me! I am lucky—these are the good moments.

GF FOOD IS EVERYWHERE! We are finding yummy GF food in soooooo many places. GF is pretty popular now, whether you have celiac or a gluten sensitivity. There are A LOT of GF products. My mom and I still read the labels pretty carefully, but there are lots of options out there. I am EXTREMELY GRATEFUL!

NICOLE THE NUTRITIONIST. I see her at the celiac support group meetings, and she is ALWAYS so reassuring that I am doing well and so happy to see me. She has been a really positive influence on my life (I'm even considering being a nutritionist when I grow up—seriously, no joke).

Thank goodness for the good moments,

PWDU
(People Who Don't Understand)

Dear Journal,

Well, even though I am adjusting, I have to be honest. There have been some moments that haven't been entirely great. I have been thinking of them as my PWDU moments—People Who Don't Understand.

There is always that person who thinks they know it all. Uggghhhhh. I cannot describe in words how annoying it is when someone thinks they know more than you (especially when it's something in reality they don't know too much about).

This is what happened today!

> FRIEND: "What exactly can't you have?" and just as I was about to answer, this OTHER FRIEND answers, "Oh, it's just flour. Anything with flour."

Inside I'm like "NNOOOOOO," but instead of screaming NNOOOOOO, I take a breath . . .

ME: "I actually can have flour just not wheat flour, rye, barley, or anything containing these three products."

PHEW!!!! **big deep breath*** It might not seem like a big deal, but I'm sort of sensitive about what people think they know and if it is actually true. I don't like people getting false or half-true information.

Here are some things I wish I could put on a billboard for all PWDU's to read:

- If you buy a bag of GF pretzels for me to eat THAT IS SOOO NICE OF YOU, but if you put them in a bowl that was not washed well, UNFORTUNATELY, THAT IS NOT OK— POSSIBLE CROSS-CONTAMINATION ISSUES.
- If I order a salad without croutons, but it comes with croutons, IT IS NOT OK TO JUST TAKE THE CROUTONS OFF. I NEED A WHOLE NEW SALAD. Again, CROSS-CONTAMINATION ISSUES. FYI, same thing for a burger on a bun. Can't just take off the gluten bun and put the burger on a GF bun … You can try, but that wouldn't be good for me.
- If it doesn't say "Gluten Free" on the packaging and it's made with natural or artificial flavors, IT'S NOT OK. I DON'T KNOW WHAT IS IN THOSE FLAVORS— GLUTEN IS A POSSIBILITY.
- If you are grilling steak or chicken that is marinated with a wheat or gluten-filled marinade and then want to grill

my food on the same grill with the same set of tongs, IT'S NOT OK. CROSS-CONTAMINATION ISSUES.

- If you're using your oven or toaster, please use tinfoil to act as a barrier between the food and the grill—that will really help—but POP-UP TOASTERS are a no-go. Definite CROSS-CONTAMINATION WITH THOSE.
- If you think celiac disease is the same as a gluten sensitivity or eating gluten free for health reasons, IT IS SIMILAR, BUT NOT THE SAME.

If your family or friends think they get it and don't, it can make you feel like a flat tire or a week-old balloon—deflated. It can be really hard when people prepare food for me and I'm not sure it was made safely. I know I can always ask to see the ingredients used and the packaging, but it's not easy. It feels rude and uncomfortable to decline, but then again I don't want to hurt my body. For the celiac-ites out there who "feel" the gluten, the intense fear about getting sick and feeling awful is definitely not worth it. Also, it's hard to say no thank you, especially if you are hungry.

> TIP: It's always a good idea to eat something before you go out and bring something with you just in case.

Having celiac disease is totally doable, if the people in your life get it. A few more PWDU moments have happened, but I'm glad to say that the good moments far outweigh the PWDU moments.

I love roses, but even the most beautiful roses have a few thorns. It's life. It's reality. It's my life. It's the average celiac-ite's reality, but I know I got this even with the PWDU moments.

NOVEMBER 19

This Gluten-Free Steak Is GREAT!

Dear Journal,

What a day! I just came home from tennis to eat a quick dinner with my cousin. As we're wolfing down our food, I hear Tyler say with serious enthusiasm, "THIS GLUTEN-FREE STEAK IS GREAT!" My parents smiled and I almost spit out my water. Tyler looked surprised. He definitely intended his comment to be complimentary, which it was, but it was funny too since all steak is pretty much gluten free. If you marinade it in a sauce that is made with wheat or gluten, then you are adding gluten to it, but it is really easy to keep the steak naturally gluten free. Tyler lives just 2 miles away from me and is over a lot. Since we keep our whole house gluten free, he has also been trying to get used to eating gluten free when he's over.

It's so fun to introduce friends and family to my food, <u>especially</u> when they enjoy it!

Not all gluten-free food is great, but that's the same deal with gluten-filled food. Anyway, Tyler was so right—that gluten-free steak was great!

Lexi

NOVEMBER 28

Potato Chip Bread Crumbs

Dear Journal,

Here's a tip … courtesy of my mother. She never did this B.C., but it has become a regular thing now. I almost never eat all the chips that she sends to school with me, and there are always leftover broken chips in the bag, so instead of tossing them Mom keeps them in a plastic bag. After the bag gets pretty full we take out a mallet and crush them—it's been a good stress release—and then she uses them as bread crumbs for chicken or in our turkey meatballs. She was thinking of creating some sort of contraption to make this process easier, though the act of smashing the chips with the mallet definitely has its perks! Mom has been really excited with this invention for weeks and mentioned it to our cousin, who suggested just putting the leftover chips in the food processor. Well, that worked better than the mallet. Goodbye to my mom's hopes for being on "Shark Tank" and getting a deal with Lori Greiner and having her contraption sell on QVC. But hello to awesome potato chip bread crumbs! (FYI: it works with pretzels, too!)

Lexi

A Picky Eater

Dear Journal,

Grandma was over today and told me this story about her friend. This friend is someone my grandma has known for more than 30 years, way longer than I've been alive, and to my grandma's surprise this friend has celiac. Even though my grandma asks me a gazillion questions, it turns out she never asked this friend questions. She just always thought this friend was a really picky eater and she left it at that. Turns out this friend was diagnosed with celiac in her early 40s. Maybe it was because celiac wasn't something people really knew a lot about or she was private, who knows the reason, but after years of knowing each other my grandma seriously just thought she was a picky eater! My grandma had no idea that her friend used to have to order gluten-free food from Canada because there was no selection in our supermarkets. Can you imagine?! Ordering food from Canada!!!!!!! I am so lucky that if I have to have this disease I have it now. All the supermarkets have an aisle, a section, something… Canada is great and all—I have cousins there—but I wouldn't want to have to order food from there.
    Phew!

Moral #1 of the story: Canada probably has really good GF food options as they have been doing it so long.

Moral #2 of the story: Don't make assumptions about your friends.

Moral #3 of the story: Grandmas talk to their friends about their grandchildren. They can't help themselves!

Lexi

JANUARY 27

Meeting Dr. Peter Green

Dear Journal,

I am in the car on my way home from New York. I just met Dr. Peter Green! Why the exclamation point you may ask? Well, I'll tell you, Journal. When I was first diagnosed, my grandma handed my mom this crumpled piece of paper. Written on it in pencil was "Dr. Peter Green, Celiac Center Columbia." Grandma's friend told her he was the "celiac expert," and when we met with Nicole she said he was her "idol."

So it seems like he is a definite celebrity in the world of celiac.

Dr. Peter Green, Celiac Center Columbia

My parents went to a meeting led by Dr. Green for parents of children with celiac. I sat in the room next door and met him when it was over. My mom, the memory keeper that she is, was bold enough to ask to snap a picture of me with him. Then she sent it to Nicole to say guess who we just met!?! In any case, my parents thought it was neat to speak with and meet Dr. Green and the other doctors he works with. They said that it's sort of like going to Nicole's celiac support groups, but this one had only parents there and a lot of doctors and the Celiac Disease Center's nutritionist. Mom said there is a real camaraderie (big word, but not a medical one this time) in talking with other parents. Everyone has their own story of how their child was diagnosed, what stage they are at, and how they're handling it. It seemed to reassure my parents that everyone does things a little differently, but there are some basic no-no's we all follow. Based on my mom's tone of voice, she seems more relaxed. I think she feels good about what we've been doing, and she got some positive feedback that we are on the right track. I guess even moms who seem like they have it all together need some reassurance sometimes!

Lexi

Anything WITH Gluten

Dear Journal,

So meeting Dr. Green and getting some positive feedback has been good—finding out there are a lot of food options has been reassuring, but yes, the whole thing has been an adjustment... I'm doing pretty well, but what I'm realizing more and more is that having celiac disease is not just an adjustment for me, but for my extended family as well. Yes, they've been supportive and many of them have even been tested for celiac—since it's a genetic disease, there is a higher likelihood it will turn up in family members.

TIP:
Family members should be tested – including relatives like your aunts, uncles, and grandparents!

Well, it turns out gluten is a non-issue for them. They can eat whatever they want, but at my house we are 100% gluten free. So when my older cousin came over to help me with science and my mother, being the "I-have-to-feed-you" type of mother, asks my cousin what he wants, his reply is "anything WITH gluten." I could see by my mom's scrunched-up face she was taken aback by his request, but kids will say it as it is, especially a 17-year-old growing boy. After my mom made him corn tortilla chips with melted cheese followed up with a couple of Hershey chocolate bars and her brownies, I realized I wasn't the only one who was adjusting. Sure my cousin could have softened his comments a bit, but it was his reality. He likes gluten, he can eat gluten, and he wanted gluten. But it is what it is. He's not going to be able to eat gluten in my house … Fortunately, he ate the chips, scarfed down the Hershey bars, and polished them off with a brownie (I'm putting Mom's amazing recipe at the end of the journal). He seemed to do just fine without the gluten, and he helped me with my science —yay for understanding dimensional analysis!

Change can be scary. Most people don't like change (FYI most people don't like dimensional analysis either), but everyone gets through it. I will too.

Lexi

FEBRUARY 1

Djokovic (jo-ka-vitch), a.k.a. Chipwich

Dear Journal,

I LOVE TENNIS. I play as much as possible! Who knew that I would have something other than a love for tennis in common with Novak Djokovic, one of the best tennis players in the world! The funniest part is that I used to have trouble saying his name. My nickname for him is "Chipwich." Well, I guess the joke is on us as neither of us are eating a Chipwich these days, not the gluten-filled kind anyway.

While he was playing a tournament I heard the sportscaster say something like "Is a gluten-free diet behind Djokovic's success?" ... I googled his story. He described himself as feeling like a "beached whale" before he stopped eating gluten. To be honest Journal, I never knew that it wasn't "normal" to feel like a "beached whale"—when you don't know what's "normal," I guess it's hard to know what's not "normal." I'm still learning, Journal!

Well, it seems that he doesn't have celiac disease, but he stopped eating gluten in 2010. After he changed what he was eating he felt a lot better (and went on to become the NUMBER 1 tennis player in the world). Truthfully, I am a HUGE Roger Federer fan—I mean he is the GOAT, I mean Greatest of All Time—but this newfound connection with Chipwich has me curious and more interested in him. The article said that his asthma and chronic fatigue decreased, and he was sleeping better and had more energy after he stopped eating gluten. I've always been a little sluggish, so maybe I will feel more energetic too once all of the gluten is wiped out of my body. I'm hoping to make the high school tennis team next year... Maybe I'll follow in Chipwich's footsteps.

"Love" Lexi (tennis pun intended)

Lexi
40

gluten
0

FEBRUARY 13

C-E-L-I-A-C: Acrostic Style

Dear Journal,

Remember when you learned about acrostic poems in elementary school? My all-time favorite one was L-E-X-I, of course...

L is for Loyal—Being a good friend

E is for Enthusiastic—Showing a lot of interest

X is for eXcellent—Really, really great

I is for Imaginative—Being creative

I was just daydreaming and doodling and made an acrostic poem for C-E-L-I-A-C... I'm trying to look at the bright side. I think if I do it enough, I will believe it more... so here it is:

C is for Careful—What celiac-ites need to be

E is for Eating—What I can still do ☺
THANKFULLY!

L is for Loving the Certified GF label

I is for Intestines—Letting my villi grow back

A is for Ability—Celiac-ites can do this

C is for Courage—One meal at a time (and
snacks, of course)

Lexi, the poet

What I've Learned This Year (EVERYONE'S GOT SOMETHING)

Dear Journal,

It's pretty wild that almost a year has passed since my diagnosis and since I started writing in you. I know it will sound a little corny to thank a journal, but it has been really helpful getting my thoughts out and processing all these changes and first experiences of being gluten free. I have family and friends that have been really supportive this year—without them this whole celiac thing would have probably been a lot harder. I learned A LOT this year (and not just from being in 8th grade), but the real-life stuff that you can't learn from a 10-pound textbook.

One of the biggest lessons I've learned is that EVERYONE'S GOT SOMETHING, whether it is celiac disease, being really shy, being overly competitive, being anxious, having eczema, or a learning disability. Everyone has something. Other people may not know what it is, but whatever that something is it DOESN'T NEED TO DEFINE WHO YOU ARE OR LIMIT YOU, unless you let it.

No one is perfect, I know that. I know I get frustrated easily, I am absolutely terrified of needles and blood, I don't like staying home alone, and sometimes I talk too much. On the other hand, I am kind, charitable, a loving daughter, sister, granddaughter, niece, cousin, and friend, a tennis player, and an avid reader of really good books that I can read over and over again (thumbs up to "The Selection Series"). My favorite color is a yellowish-green and I love lemony desserts and macaroons, taking creative photos, designing fashions, and watching reality cooking shows (even if they are filled with gluten products) and "The Amazing Race." Oh, and I have celiac disease. Yes, it is part of who I am, but that's the point—it's not the only part of who I am. Does it affect me every day? Yes, but if I'm prepared (thanks, Girl Scout motto—did I mention I'm a Girl Scout, too?) and think ahead, I can not only manage living with celiac disease, I can thrive. Bam.

Lexi

APRIL 7

I'm Turning 14— Seeing the Pediatrician Again

Dear Journal,

It's been one year since I saw my pediatrician at my last well checkup appointment (you know, the one that didn't turn out so "well"). I used to CRY and SCREAM when I saw him—yes I was really little at the time, but I was not a fan of this man who ordered shots for me. (Have I mentioned how I feel about shots???) My mom tried everything to make me like him. She even used to put a photo of him on our refrigerator along- side the magazine cutouts of Disney princesses and photos of grandparents to make him seem just like a loved member of the family. We would bake for him and visit his office when I didn't even have an appointment... Well, fast forward a decade, and I definitely don't scream anymore when I see him, but I have a host of other feelings, some nerves, but mostly gratitude.

Remember my well checkup appointment from my very first entry? Well, I found out that my mom spoke to the pediatrician alone in his office right after the appointment. She expressed

73

her concern about my growth and asked if we should just check things out to be on the safe side. For a few years he had said to her, "You aren't so big yourself," and he didn't think there was any need to be concerned. So I'm really grateful he ordered the bloodwork last year. I'm also grateful that he included the test for celiac disease. That was not on my mom's radar at all—she just wanted confirmation I was OK. Despite my extreme hatred for anything related to blood tests, I am very, very thankful he ordered them.

At my well checkup today I grew 3 inches since last year, more than I've grown in recent years, and I'm back on my growth chart—I'm moving in the right direction. The doctor seemed pleased. Me too!—I'm edging closer to sitting in the front passenger seat of the car safely, so if the air bag deploys, it won't completely smush me! Yes, he told me I should be at least 5 feet tall and 100 pounds to sit in the front—he is "conservative" and my mom listens, so being a front-seat passenger is definitely not happening yet . . .

I'll never know if my growth would have been different if we'd figured out this celiac thing earlier, but I'm really doing ok. Some people have symptoms for years, and they don't figure it out for a long time. What I am realizing is that celiac has been around for a long time, but was not something doctors tested for. Now that they're testing more for it, more people are being identified with it and can feel better by changing their food. It's pretty cool to have a disease that doesn't require medicine, therapies, or operations—I get to eat good food to nourish me. Would I like to go to a party, restaurant, or friend's house and just eat anything I wanted? Sure. I'd be lying if I said I didn't, but I just need to make some adjustments. I have choices and I can live with that. There are a lot of things that go wrong in life, a lot of things that people have to live with. I CAN DO THIS.

Lexi

Camping Gluten-Free Style

Dear Journal,

Remember that raffle my dad entered at the Gluten Free Expo to go to a camp for a weekend!? Well, we won! We never win anything, ok. We never really enter raffles, but we did this time. I am in the bunk now writing to you! We just finished jet skiing, paddle boarding, and going on the banana boat. Somehow my hearing is still intact even though my mother was literally screaming her brains out! So this place is a regular camp, but they have a dedicated gluten-free kitchen and EVERYONE here this weekend is eating gluten free. We've gone to a couple of lectures by doctors specializing in celiac disease. It's been really interesting meeting so many different people. EVERYONE HAS A STORY, and what's weird is that everyone's story is somehow different, but they're all similar at the same time. And no matter how anyone's story begins, the ending is always the same: NO GLUTEN!

Off to the bonfire to make s'mores! Love this camp!

Lexi

MAY 12

The One-Year Blood Test

Dear Journal,

I wouldn't say it was smooth sailing with the phlebotomist, but it was definitely better than before. I still used the lidocaine, I still stood at the door and required A LOT of coaxing by my mom to sit in the chair, but I didn't scream this time. No hearing loss for the phlebotomist—yes, there are miracles—and now we wait for the results. This time I don't think I'll forget about waiting for them. I'm hopeful and nervous. Wish me luck, Journal.

Lexi

MAY 21

The G.I. Guy Again

Dear Journal,

I felt like I walked into the G.I. Guy's office a little taller this year. Not just literally, as I know I've grown in the physical sense, but I've also grown by learning and doing so much. I have followed his GF prescription to a tee. I am proud of myself, and I found out my efforts have paid off. The G.I. Guy reviewed my bloodwork, and it was clear that my numbers were "not normal," but they were SOOOOOO much better than last year, and I am clearly moving in the right direction. He also reviewed the EMA blood test, which is a special test that can help diagnose celiac. A positive result means you have celiac, but a negative result doesn't mean you DON'T have it—the test just might not be picking it up. I know, it's kinda strange. Anyway, my result was positive, which means I do have celiac. We knew I had celiac, but this gave further credence to all of it—

My mom teared up. She has put on a good game face this year and has been unbelievable, but I know this was a change not only for me, but for my whole family. The G.I. Guy was supportive and encouraged me to keep up with what I was doing, and he didn't call me ABNORMAL this time around, which I was very happy about!

Lexi

Why I Am Grateful

Dear Journal,

#1 Celiac disease can lead to A LOT of health issues later in life if it's untreated. Luckily, we found out I had it early. This way I can learn what is safe for me to eat and what isn't, and it will set me up for a healthier life down the road. Sometimes it's hard to think "BIG PICTURE." Seriously, I am a newly minted teenager. But if I look ahead to my aunt having a baby or my mom having run a half-marathon or my grandparents being active playing tennis and golf and traveling into their 60s and 70s, I want to be healthy too and be able to do whatever I want without having to worry if my health is compromised. My mom has told me you can't control everything in life, but you can make good decisions, be responsible and be in charge of how you respond to situations. I am choosing to make healthy decisions for myself and look at the glass totally full instead of half full. (Don't forget the air in the glass. I love that saying—thanks, Mrs. Weakly.)

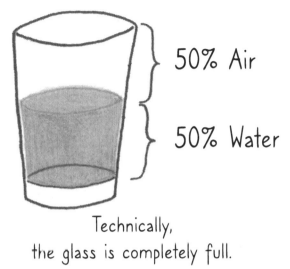

50% Air

50% Water

Technically,
the glass is completely full.

On that note, I am grateful. Yes I have celiac disease, but I really believe that it is just one part of who I am. I am a lot bigger, stronger, and braver than before I was diagnosed. I can handle it, and when I have questions or concerns, there is a lot of support in the Land of Lexi. Yes, I really am lucky.

#2 I haven't written about my sister until right now. SURPRISE! I have an identical twin, who was diagnosed with celiac just when I was. I am grateful that I have had her to go through this with. We have shared pretty much everything in life literally from the beginning—celiac, too. I bet you didn't see that one coming, Journal! Pretty sneaky! I haven't written about her yet because I wanted to give myself a chance to process this change in my life through my own eyes, with my own thoughts and my own feelings. I think I did that, but I'd have to say she is my best friend, and it has been comforting to know that we have been in this together.

I know not everyone has a twin or even a brother or sister to navigate the ups and downs in life, but I guess if I didn't, I would still do what I did this past year—

- get a journal
- talk to a couple of good friends
- get a nutritionist
- go to a local support group
- talk to my mom or dad—parents aren't as weird as books and movies make them seem, at least not all of the time.

Even when I feel alone with this, even with having a sister who has it too, I know that I'm not alone. Nobody is fully alone if you can surround yourself with people you love and trust.

> FUN FACT courtesy of my mom: For every 133 people you meet, at least 1 of them has celiac, so there are probably a few people in my grade who have it or just don't know it yet.

#3 I am big-time grateful for ALL of the GF products on the market. Whether it is the GF aisle in the supermarket, the GF bakery we go to, or the camp I'm going to with my Girl Scout troop for our overnight this year that has a dedicated GF kitchen, so much of society gets it, and I have plenty of choices. FOR THAT, I AM EXTREMELY GRATEFUL!

This has been my first year with celiac. I look forward to seeing what will get easier over time. I know I'll feel bummed out, even left out sometimes when I can't eat what everyone else is, but I'm going to focus on the good stuff—the people I'm with, the experiences I can have, and the food I can eat. Thanks for listening, Journal! I smell cheesy baked ziti downstairs for dinner—I want to get there before my sister eats it all!

XOXO, Lexi

A MOTHER'S PERSPECTIVE

by Lori Akawie Katzman, Psy.D.

Through My Eyes

It's been a little over four years since my daughters were diagnosed with celiac disease. As with most situations in life, there
have been ups and there have been downs. There have been
really supportive and empathetic comments, and there have been
really dismissive and hurtful ones. In the end, the comments
that are most important are those that are going through my
daughters' minds—what they are saying to themselves, how
they are coping, how they're navigating this life change in the
house and out of the house today, tomorrow, and every day
after that.

So far I've managed their in-house eating really well, but I
have to say out of the house has been hands-down the hardest
part of this life change. Within the refuge of my own kitchen
I know what they are eating is safe for them, but I have to say
my struggle is trusting outside establishments to prepare their
food safely. Initially, I reverted to strategies from their infant/
toddler years, bringing food with me from home whenever we

were on the go. The notion of my kids being deprived, missing out, or not having something safe to eat that is on par with what is being served to others was unacceptable to me, so if I could provide what they needed and deserved, I would tow a bag with me without a second thought. It was just my new normal. But now that they are seventeen, going out with their friends and soon enough off to college, my extra bag has become their bag, my preparation is becoming their responsibility, and my apprehension to have them eat out is being lessened one meal at a time.

But, I've been scared … When I learned my kids had this disease with an "atypical" presentation, without the well-known gastrointestinal symptoms, the constant conundrum in my head was how will I know if we mess up and contaminate them? How will we know if they get "glutened"? Since they might not show any symptoms, our fears and vigilance about getting "glutened" are different from those of other "celiac-ites." I don't envy their peers with celiac disease who experience severe symptoms when contaminated. They truly suffer by physically feeling awful, not to mention the damage that is occurring to their small intestine. My kids, as far as I know, suffer in silence, damaging their small intestine but not knowing it. So whether they feel the gluten or not, the choice is clear. Like all people with celiac disease, they have to be really, really careful.

On the other hand, part of raising kids is to foster independence, growth, and the ability to figure out how to thrive in this crazy, unpredictable world. I guess we look at celiac disease like an allergy to something like dairy or nuts (though it's not, that is the simple explanation that is best understood by the "outside world"). I know gluten won't cause my kids to go into anaphylactic shock, but they do have to be very thoughtful not only about what they eat, but how it is prepared.

Events, parties, athletics, hangouts big and small all involve food in some way, so there is no ignoring it or hiding it—celiac disease has to be managed and lived with daily. During year one they handled this life transition with a ridiculous amount of grace, and years two and three continued to go pretty well. Now we are through year four. Their serology numbers are a lot lower, but still not in the normal range. I find this incredibly frustrating. I am the type of person who, if you tell me what to do, I will follow the rules and then expect not only results, but the maximum results. Thanks to some caring doctors in my life, I have been advised not to get caught up in a number, but to look at their clinical picture as a whole: they have grown. If I really want to know if any intestinal damage persists, they would have to go through with the endoscopy, which continues to be a no-go for them. They astutely point out to me that whether there is damage or not, the follow-up is the same—life-long gluten free. So it is what it is. At some point, I recognized that "everyone's got something," and this happened to be our "something." This is our new normal, and every day, month, and year they will get better at handling it.

As Lexi says, they have celiac disease, but in no way does it define who they are.

I do believe my daughters—all the "Lexis" and all the other "celiac-ites" out there can handle this.

You got this!

ADDITIONAL RESOURCES

by Hallie, Rayna, and Lori Katzman

The Decision to Go Gluten Free Without the Biopsy

Being diagnosed without the "gold standard" biopsy is not the suggested approach in the United States. The decision whether or not to have an endoscopy in order to perform a biopsy is for you to come to as a family and especially under the medical supervision of a physician who is a celiac disease expert. We made our choice based on symptomatology, bloodwork, and guidance from our doctors.

Some information from the University of Chicago's Celiac Disease Center website further helped us with this decision. In their Frequently Answered Questions section appears the following question and answer dated December 29, 2012:

Q: Will the biopsy continue to be the gold standard for diagnosis?

A: It's very likely that the biopsy will remain the gold standard for years to come; approximately 90 percent of new cases are diagnosed using an endoscopic biopsy as part of the diagnosis. Only in rare cases is a diagnosis made without a biopsy as part of the diagnosis. In these rare cases a patient must have at least one of the genes for celiac disease, tTG and EMA elevated more than 10x normal, and a positive response to a gluten-free diet. Those who should receive a biopsy to diagnose celiac disease include those with:

- Positive antibody blood test prior to starting a gluten-free diet.
- Unexplained iron deficiency anemia not responding to therapy.
- Early osteoporosis.
- Neuropathy/ataxia.

More recently, in July 2017, the website Beyond Celiac published an article describing a large-scale international study that suggested that children may not need a biopsy to be diagnosed with celiac disease. Specific factors must be considered, and again it is recommended that this decision be made in concert with a physician knowledgeable about the disease.

At the end of the day, foregoing the biopsy was a decision that worked for our family. We encourage you to meet with your own physician and determine what makes sense given your unique situation.

OUR FOOD LIST
(A Work in Progress)

TIP: always read the labels—even when labeled GF!

Words to watch out for on ingredient labels	What I can have
barley	almond flour
bulgur	amaranth
couscous	arrowroot
farina	beans
faro	buckwheat
Kamut (Khorasan wheat)	corn
malt (or anything that begins with malt)	corn flour

OUR FOOD LIST (A WORK IN PROGRESS)

Words to watch out for on ingredient labels ☹	What I can have ☺
matzah	gluten-free oats (avoid these for the first year)
oats	
rye	maltodextrin is ok if the package says it is GF
seitan	
semolina	millet
spelt	potatoes
tabbouleh	quinoa
triticale	rice
wheat	rice flour
wheat flour	sorghum
wheat germ	soy
	tapioca
	taro
	teff
	xanthan gum
	yeast

BIG Word Definitions

anemia — A condition in which a person has fewer red blood cells than normal. A low red cell count could be caused by a few different situations: 1) Red blood cells are being lost; 2) The body is producing red blood cells more slowly than it should; or 3) The body is destroying red blood cells. Anemia is a very common symptom of celiac disease. Anemia and celiac disease often appear together because celiac interferes with the absorption of nutrients from food, and anemia can be caused by a lack of iron, folic acid, or vitamin B12. (May 29)

antecubital space — The area of your arm near the crease of your elbow. It is the most commonly used space to draw blood from because the veins are typically large in that area. (October 14)

autoimmune condition — A disease that causes the body to produce antibodies that attack its own tissues, leading to the deterioration and in some cases the destruction of such tissue. (August 16)

biopsy — Removing tissue, cells, or fluids from a body to examine them. During an endoscopy to confirm the celiac disease diagnosis, a doctor takes sample tissues from different parts of the small intestine. A biopsy is generally considered the gold standard in diagnosing celiac disease. (May 17)

camaraderie – Friendly and positive feelings that a group of people have for each other. (January 27)

celiac disease – A genetic autoimmune disease. "Genetic" means it runs in families. (See "autoimmune disorder" above.) Celiac disease is not an allergy. When you have celiac disease, your body responds negatively to gluten. There are more than 200 symptoms that can be present when you have celiac disease. (May 11)

cross-contamination – When a contaminant is unintentionally transferred from one substance or surface to another. Cross-contamination can occur when gluten comes into contact with gluten-free food and can happen at home or when eating out. It is typically easier to prevent cross-contamination at home using basic guidelines, such as keeping hands, utensils, cutting boards, and colanders clean, and then having duplicates of items you use regularly. When eating out, pay particular attention to the oil used to fry foods and the use of flour in food, as well as whether certain cooking equipment is easy to clean (nonporous equipment is easier to clean than porous). (May 20, June 11, August 16, and November 17)

EMA – A blood test that looks for the endomysial antibodies. EMA is a highly specific test for the presence of celiac disease. If the test is positive, virtually 100 percent of the time the person will have celiac disease. However, some people with celiac disease may not be positive for EMA. The test is expensive, time-consuming, and qualitative, which means the results can be difficult to interpret. It's best used as an additional test to the routine tTG-IgA test. (May 21)

endoscopy – Is not surgery! It's a way for your doctor to see what your small intestine looks like. The doctor uses a flexible tube with a light and camera attached to it. The camera images are projected onto a TV monitor so the doctor can see inside the intestine. (May 2 and May 17)

gastroenterologist – A doctor who studies diseases of the stomach and intestinal tract. A pediatric gastroenterologist specializes in treating infants through children in their teen years who have digestive, liver, or nutritional problems. (May 2)

gluten – A protein found in wheat, rye, and barley. This protein can cause a physical reaction in certain people, particularly those who have celiac disease. Some typical foods that contain gluten are pizza, bread, cakes, and cereal. (May 4)

HLA-DQ8 and HLA-DQ2 genes – The two genes found in people who have celiac disease. Because celiac is genetically linked, a person needs to have certain genes to have the disease. DQ2 is the most common gene found in people with celiac; the other is DQ8. If you have HLA-DQ8 combined with HLA-DQ2, then your risk to develop celiac disease is even higher—about fourteen times that of the general population. (May 17)

lidocaine – A topical anesthetic cream that works by numbing the surface of the skin for a short period of time. It can be applied before getting your blood drawn. It helps to lessen the perceived pain; however, you may still feel some pressure or touch. (April 24)

osteoporosis – A medical condition in which the bones become brittle and fragile from loss of tissue, typically as a result of hormonal changes or deficiency of calcium or vitamin D. People who have celiac disease are more at risk for the main complication of osteoporosis, which is fractures. Up to 75 percent of newly diagnosed patients with celiac disease have some bone loss. (May 29)

percentile – A number on a scale of 100 that compares something to a larger group. Percentiles are used to show your growth compared to other people the same age as you. You can have percentiles for how tall you are and how much you weigh. Higher numbers (closer to 100) indicate a larger or taller child, and lower numbers (closer to 0) indicate a smaller or shorter child. For example, a girl in the 75th percentile for weight would be larger than 75 girls out of 100 and smaller than 25 girls out of 100. These numbers allow a doctor to compare your height to your weight to determine proportionate growth. A child with 90th-percentile weight and 25th-percentile height is probably carrying too much weight for her height, whereas a child in the 50th percentiles for both height and weight has an even proportion. (April 21)

phlebotomist – A medical professional who draws blood for testing or transfusions. (Fortunately, some phlebotomists are specifically trained to work with children. They are patient, kind, and informative and make the process of drawing blood as easy as possible.) The phlebotomist works in a medical office or hospital and sends the blood to a lab for testing. (April 24)

small intestine – Part of the digestive system, the small intestine receives food from the stomach and continues to break it down so all the nutrients the body needs can be absorbed. (May 11 and May 18)

villi – Tiny finger-like structures that cover the inner surface of the small intestine and absorb nutrients. All over the villi are microvilli, even tinier "fingers" that maximize absorption. (May 4, May 11, and May 18)

Eating Out?
Typical Questions to Ask
at the Restaurant

TIP: Call ahead and speak to a manager (not during busy meal times) before choosing a restaurant. If that isn't possible, speak to the waiter or manager when you arrive.

- Do you have a gluten-free menu?
- Do you use separate utensils when preparing the food?
- Do you have a dedicated fryer for french fries?
- Do you know what cross-contamination is? How do you avoid it? For instance, is there a separate area of the kitchen allotted to prepare gluten-free food safely?
- Are there breadcrumbs in your meatballs or hamburgers?
- Is the meal marinated? If so, do you know if there is gluten in the marinade or any flour? Do you have any chicken or meat that is not already marinated?
- Is your soy sauce gluten free?
- Do you grill fish or chicken on a grill that may have just been used to grill something like focaccia bread? If so, do

you clean the grill? Can you use foil or a separate pan to grill my food?

- Is there a flour coating on the food or pans when cooking?
- Do you use clean water when making the gluten-free pasta?
- Do you use flour to thicken sauces, gravies, or soups?
- When making eggs or omelettes do you add flour or pancake batter?
- When making eggs or omelettes do you use a different pan than used when making pancakes?

Semi-Homemade Brownies

(Pure deliciousness—
All GF and NON-GF friends LOVE them)

Ingredients:

- King Arthur Gluten Free Brownie Mix (1 box)
- Immaculate Gluten Free Chocolate Chunk Cookie Dough (9 cookies)
- Enjoy Life Semi-Sweet Chocolate Mini Chips (1/2 cup)
- Elyon Marshmallows (8 large, broken into smaller pieces)

Directions:

1) Put a piece of tinfoil in the bottom of a 9×9-inch baking pan.
2) Spray the tinfoil with Pam Simply Coconut Oil (labeled GF).
3) Flatten the cookies to form the bottom layer.
4) Make the brownie mix as indicated on the box.
5) Add the mini chocolate chips and marshmallows to the brownie mix.
6) Mix the batter well and pour onto the layer of cookie dough.
7) Bake as indicated in the brownie directions and check for doneness. The brownies might need a few extra minutes of baking time due to the added ingredients (approximately 45–50 minutes). Please note these brownies tend to be more fudge-like than cake-like.

Note: Ingredients can typically be found in Whole Foods and large regional chain supermarkets.

Start Your Own Journal

EVERYONE'S GOT SOMETHING:
My Experiences Living (with Celiac Disease and Everything Else.)

Write, draw—whatever works for you!
Find a pen, pencil, or marker and put it to paper.

THIS IS FOR YOU.
Get it out and work with what you've got.

Keep in mind all responses
DO NOT have to be related to celiac disease.

This is part of you,
NOT all of you.

My name is

_____

I'm in _____ grade, and I'm _____ years old.

I love to play

_____

_____

_____

I found out I had celiac disease when I was

_____

The hardest thing about having celiac disease is

_____

_____

_____

_____

_____

_____

The best thing about finding out I had celiac disease is

_____

_____

_____

_____

_____

_____

My favorite foods to eat are

_____

_____

_____

I really miss

_____

_____

_____

_____

The person (or people) who has really helped me figure out the gluten-free world is

_____

_____

My top 3 wishes are

_____

_____

_____

I am grateful for (remember, it doesn't have to be something food related)

_____

_____

_____

_____

_____

_____

It really bothers me when

_____

_____

_____

_____

_____

_____

_____

My favorite places to eat are

_____

_____

_____

Favorite activities after school are

_____

_____

_____

From having celiac disease, I've learned that I

_____

_____

_____

_____

_____

I love when

_____

_____

_____

_____

_____

Over the summer I love to

_____

_____

_____

_____

My (sister/brother/friend) has been
- ○ supportive
- ○ caring
- ○ indifferent
- ○ uncaring
- ○ all of the above at different times
- ○ none of the above. I would really describe that person as

_____

_____

_____

If I could give one piece of advice to another kid who has celiac disease, I would tell them

_____

_____

_____

_____

_____

_____

_____

When I get older, I want to

_____

_____

_____

_____

_____

Make an acrostic poem with your name (remember February 13).

_____

_____

_____

_____

_____

_____

_____

_____

We hope starting your own journal
has been helpful and fun!

108

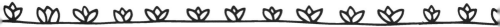

Lexi has hereby declared you an . . .

Honorary
Celiac-ite

You got this!

ACKNOWLEDGMENTS

In addition to our ridiculously supportive family and friends, the following people and establishments truly made a difference in our lives during our first year after being diagnosed.

A simple thank you does not seem adequate, so how about a REALLY, REALLY BIG THANK YOU!!!!

Dr. Laurence D. Gruenwald, MD, Pediatrician
Dr. Kenneth M. Miller, MD, Gastroenterologist
Dr. Francis P. Sunaryo, MD, Pediatric Gastroenterologist
Nicole Yelton, RD, LDN, CNHP
Sheryl Harpel, Founder of Gluten Free Friends, LLC
Lillian Duggan, Editor
Antonn Park, Blue Flower Editing
Gloriously Gluten Free in Stirling, NJ
Pascarella Bros. Deli in Chatham, NJ and Morristown, NJ
The Squirrel and the Bee in Short Hills, NJ
Legal Seafood in Short Hills, NJ
Camp Nah-Jee-Wah in Milford, PA

Lori, Hallie, and Rayna Katzman
Photo by: Stephen Taylor - Portrait Artist

Authors

Hallie Katzman and Rayna Katzman are now seniors at Millburn High School, co-captains of the varsity tennis team, and members of the Peer Leadership Program. They also participated in the AP/Honors Art Portfolio Program. Outside of tennis, both Rayna and Hallie love to read, spend time with their friends and family, and watch episodes of "The Amazing Race." Along with two other high school students, they started the Food Sensitivities Awareness Club at Millburn High School and also have become Celiac Student Ambassadors through the Celiac Disease Foundation. Diagnosed with celiac disease just a few weeks after turning thirteen and celebrating their b'not mitzvah, they have faced this life change with lots of questions, optimism, grace, and a positive attitude. They love to experiment in the kitchen and create gluten-free meals and desserts. They get a kick out of it when company is so surprised that their food is actually really good. And important to note: lidocaine and earmuffs for the phlebotomist are NO longer required for annual blood tests—that's major progress!

Lori Akawie Katzman, Psy.D., is the mother of Rayna and Hallie and wife of twenty years to Adam. After more than a decade volunteering in her daughters' schools, the local community, and at her synagogue, Lori returned to work as a clinical psychologist. She is currently working with older adults in a continuing care retirement community in New Jersey and continues to volunteer in her community. The family resides in Short Hills, New Jersey, with their dog, Sophie.

SOURCES

American College of Gastroenterology (website). "What Is a Gastroenterologist?" www.patients.gi.org/what-is-a-gastroenterologist/. Accessed 8 Dec. 2016.

Anderson, Jane. "HLA-DQ2: The Primary Celiac Disease Gene." Very Well Health (website). www.verywellhealth.com/hla-dq2-the-primary-celiac-disease-gene-562569. Accessed 8 Dec. 2017.

Bjarnadottir, Adda. "What Is Gluten, and Why Is It Bad for Some People?" Medical News Today (website). www.medicalnewstoday.com/articles/318606.php. Accessed 3 June 2017.

Calgary Laboratory Services (website). "Blood Collection Site Selection." www.calgarylabservices.com/education-research/medical-professionals-education/lab-101/blood-collection/site-selection.aspx. Accessed 9 Aug. 2018.

Celiac Disease Foundation (website). "What Is Celiac Disease?" www.celiac.org/celiac-disease/understanding-celiac-disease-2/what-is-celiac-disease/. Accessed 8 Dec. 2017.

Dr. Numb (website). "Lidocaine Cream Information." www.drnumb.com/lidocaine-cream/. Accessed 10 Sept. 2016.

Encyclopedia Britannica. "Villus." www.britannica.com/science/villus. Accessed 9 Aug. 2018.

Green, Peter H.R., and Rory Jones. Celiac Disease: A Hidden Epidemic. HarperCollins Publishers, 2016.

Hatter, Kathryn. "What Do the Percentiles on Child Growth Charts Mean?" Livestrong.com. www.livestrong.com/article/262492-what-do-the-percentiles-on-child-growth-charts-mean/. Accessed 13 June 2017.

Hoffman, Matthew. "Picture of the Intestines." WebMD. www.webmd.com/digestive-disorders/picture-of-the-intestines#1. Accessed 10 Aug. 2016.

Nevares, Alana M., and Robert Larner. "Overview of Autoimmune Disorders of Connective Tissue." Merck Manual (website), Merck & Co., Inc. www.merckmanuals.com/home/bone,-joint,-and-muscle-disorders/autoimmune-disorders-of-connective-tissue/overview-of-autoimmune-disorders-of-connective-tissue. Accessed 9 Aug. 2018.

Ratner, Amy. "Children May Not Need a Biopsy for Celiac Disease Diagnosis." Beyond Celiac (website). www.beyondceliac.org/research-news/View-Research-News/1394/postid--83474/?utm_content57265364&utm_

medium=social&utm_source=facebook. Accessed 7 July 2017.

Santiago, Andrea Clement. "How to Become a Phlebotomist." Very Well Health, https://www.verywellhealth.com/what-is-a-phlebotomist-1736261. Accessed 27 Feb. 2018.

UChicago Medicine Celiac Disease Center (website). "Celiac Answer Bank." www.cureceliacdisease.org/faq/will-th e-biopsy-continue-to-be-the-gold-standard-for-diagnosis/. Accessed 26 Feb. 2018.

WebMD. "Digestive Diseases and Endoscopy." www.webmd.com/digestive-disorders/digestive-diseases-endoscopy#1. Accessed 13 June 2017.

Werkstetter, K. J., et. al. "Accuracy in Diagnosis of Celiac Disease without Biopsies in Clinical Practice." *Gastroenterology*. www.gastrojournal.org/article/S0016-5085(17)35736-0/fulltext. Accessed 12 Oct. 2017.

Yates, Amber. "An Overview of Anemia." Very Well Health (website). www.verywellhealth.com/anemia-4014497. Accessed 4 Aug. 2016.

Made in the USA
Middletown, DE
15 March 2023